DIDDLE DIDDLE
Red Hot Fiddle

Patricia Powell

Illustrated by

Nikki N. Metrejean

Nikki Metrigian

FLY HIGH MUSIC HALL

THE RADIANT
and
FLY HIGH MUSIC HALL
present

Diddle Diddle Red Hot Fiddl

starring

DULAC
and
THE WHIRL CLASS CATS

DIRECTED BY
PATRICIA
POWELL

SETS BY
NIKKI N.
METREJEAN

Showtime
8:00 PM

TONIGHTS
PERFORMANCE
DEDICATED
TO
LENNO
PEACEMAKER
EXTRA ORDINEM

THE RADIANT PUBLISHING COMPANY

Thibodaux, Louisiana
U.S.A.

Copyright© 1990 by Patricia Powell

Tales from THE RADIANT, Dr. Roux, Dulac, Dat Cat, Whirl Class Cats, and associated character names and likenesses are trademarks of Patricia Powell. All rights reserved.

Order Information for this and other books and T-Shirts and requests for permission to make copies of any part of the work should be mailed to: The RADIANT Publishing Company, Post Office Drawer 796, Thibodaux, Louisiana 70302.

Thank You Teddy Baudoin and Laurie Daigle of The New Post, Ltd. and Lessie Falgout!

International Standard Book Number   0-944512-01-1
Library of Congress Catalog Card Number   89-063795

DIDDLE DIDDLE
Red Hot Fiddle

created and written by
Patricia Powell

Illustrated by
Nikki Metrejean

0233606

"Now I'm Dulac, dat Cajun Cat,
Dat Cajun Cat from down Dulac!
So take a peek - 'cause I'm unique;
I'm a left-paw-girl-who's-glad cat!
A pat-'em-on-da-back cat!
I flex my claws 'cause deez here paws
Are always pouncin' back!" WHACK!!
"Somehow I'm always catchin' flak;
But I'm a soft an' lovable Cajun Cat!
Ax* Big Mamou, she'll tell you true:
I'm a dawlin' cat who pounces back,
Her dawlin' cat from down Dulac!"

Ax   ask

Dulac Cat and little Chu-Chut kitty
Have danced their way to Fly High City.
"Our friends will join us in da talent show;
We'll kick up our heels to da zydeco!*
We've polished our taps in da practice trials;
Want to win Grand Prize an' knock 'em in da aisles!"
The cats wear costumes sewn by Big Mamou;
Ruffles and feathers are fluffin' frou-frou!*
And magic glitter flickers on to each kitty whisker;
"A gar-on-tee notes won't crack an' paws won't blister!
By the time dis star-studded night is gone
Each act but one will be a 'gone paw-can!' "
Now chimes strike eight o'clock, house lights grow dim.
The Master of Ceremonies roars, "Let the show begin!!"
Drums roll like thunder, the curtains are pulled back;
Eyes stick like glue to a stage that's thick with black!
Listen to Big Mamou as she introduces you
To her dawlin' dancin' daughter Dulac Cat:
    "She's my pat-on-the-back cat!
    A rooty-tooty jazz cat!
    What you t'ink of that, cats?"
Then Mamou turns to whisper to dawlin' Dulac's pack,
"Get out there and whirl!" She gives each cat a SMACK!
"Dance like the monkeys down at Audubon Zoo,
An' when the judges name a winner,
They'll all ax for you!!"
Now tapping out the music with her sooty little foot
And patting each cat, Dulac nudges Chu-Chut!
They strut onto the stage in a neat little row -
T-Bone and Wink with their slippers tied just so;
Magnolia follows, her tummy stuffed with grits,
Joining Tux and P.H.Dee a-puttin' on the ritz!

zydeco	*Cajun music*
frou-frou	*fussy*

Cross the diddle-diddle fiddle slides Dulac's red-hot bow
And the cats cut loose and glide across the flo'!
They spin on their heads and swirl on their toes,
While Tux Cat twirls an umbrella on his nose!
     "I'm Dulac, dat Cajun Cat,
     Dat Cajun Cat from down Dulac!
     We're pat-on-da-back cats!
     Rooty-tooty jazz cats!
     Swamp-bustin' - glad cats!
     Whatcha t'ink a dat, cats?"
On top of Tux's umbrella, Chu-Chut's spin is dizzy;
The Cajun fiddle's smokin', - the crowd is in a tizzy!
Then down the aisle they tap an old soft-shoe;
"Ladies and gentlemen, please! On with act two!!"
Ne☆n Le☆n, with hair slick and jeans sleek -
He's a handsome star and a guitar freak -
Leaps from the dark into the bright spotlight!
Diamond sweatdrops upon his brow
Drip down his chin and somehow
Pop! SNAP! CRACKLE! BOP! Tiny neon shocks
Light up his whiskers and his high-tech socks!
Then he jumpstarts his whizz guitar
And a blast of sound makes windows jar!!

     "I'm the rock 'n roll king of hearts!
     I get a charge out of raspberry tarts!
     I blink everytime that I cough!
     Blues ooze from my shoes!
     I glow when I snooze!
     Whoopie! I can't turn myself off!"

On the last neutron chord, Le☆n tosses his tie
Clear to the balcony on the very first try.
"I'm the brightest cat I know!!
I glitter! I gleam!! I glow!!!"
As the last blink of Ne☆n dances from view
The announcement is made, "Act three follows two!"

Little Peaches and Auntie cycle in hand in hand;
A piano is waiting, a fat baby grand.
For this fine duet, Peaches climbs on top to sit,
And on the bench, her Auntie fidgets a bit.
Auntie Litter clears her throat,
And strikes a clear first note:
"M-m-m-m-y niece is quite a Peach,
Always just beyond my reach;
A gritty, pretty kitty prodigy!!
She keeps me in a whirl, this sweetheart of a girl!
Fiddle-de-dee!! She's just like me!!"
To the roar of the crowd, one hundred decibels loud,
Peaches squares her shoulders looking proud:
  "If you see a Peach
  In the tip, tip, tip, tip,
  Top, top, top of the tree . . .
  Fiddle-de-dee!! It's Me!!
  And if you shake that tree
  You won't shake me!!
  No sir-r-r-eee!! 'Cuz I'm me!!"
Auntie Litter lifts her chin and begins to sing again:
"Peach is purr-fect, well almost!
All her talents I can boast,
But there's one thing I must confess!
Her room is a frightful mess!!
I'm always in a swivet, hanging clothes upon a rivet,
Cleaning closets, dusting trivets,
While my Peaches sings and pivots
On her toe, and with each pivot
She whirls a messy divot!!
Meow!! She leaves me in a swivet!!"

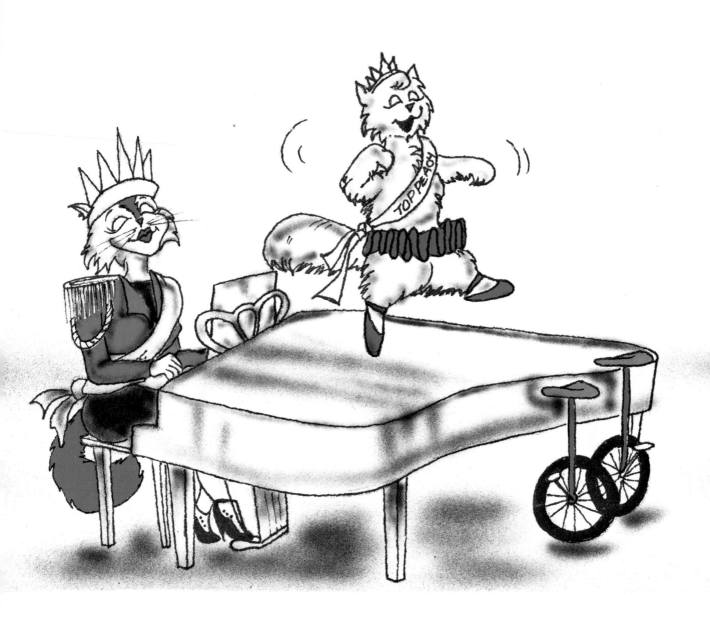

"Give me a break! Next time I wake
I hope my little sweet
Has learned to keep her life real neat!!
Then she'd be purr-fect!! Absolutely purr-fect!!
Fiddle-de-dee!! Just like me!!"
Rubbing the dimple on her chin,
Peaches breaks into a grin:
        "Oh! Fiddle-de-dee! Don't pick on me!
        I'm in your family tree!!
        Where I'm supposed to be! Fiddle-de-dee!"

Then off the stage Auntie and Peaches bounce;
"Ladies and gentlemen! We're glad to announce,
Grand Prize goes," - there's a 'paws', "to Dulac's troupe!"
The judges agree with a jubilant whoop!
"The prize is a trip to the city of your choice!"
The classy cats echo in a Cajun voice,
"Siamese cats would choose Chinese silk,
But deez here cats want Moss Cow milk!!"
"Now I'm Dulac, dat Cajun Cat,
Dat Cajun Cat from down Dulac!
And I want the other superstars to come along
To dance their dance and sing their song!
Together we can tour as The Whirl Class Cats!
We can entertain the Cow and chase away the rats!"

"Let's pack our frills and make a snappy
Trip to Moo Meadows to make the Moss Cow happy!"
And so it is set that each starring kitty
Will skoot away to the shining Creamland City.
Auntie Litter arranges the traveling plans
And they pile their bags in two Whirl Class vans.
"Uncle Rhatt is waiting at the Fly High port;
He's a Fly High pilot of the grandest sort!"
"Rat????" shriek the cats! "Who on earth is rat?
For a pesky mouse, we do NOT roll out the mat!!"
"Tsk! He's Rhatt!" explains Auntie, "the Fly High cat!
There's nothing pesky or bad about that!"
"Every dirty little rat is a dirty little brat!!
There! That's the horrible thing about that!!"

"Well, my little kittens, this Rhatt is a cat!
Rhatt Butluh! Captain Butluh in a Fly High hat!!"
Captain Butluh boards the cats on a Fly High rig
With woofers and tweeters for their Old World gig.
Le☆n dresses fancy! "I'm wearing boots made of 'gator
On tour to take Mossy a juicy sweet purr-tater!"
Dulac meows, "Want to see Moss Cow wit' da big glass nose,
Dance Da-Dulac-Dat around da big red post!"
"That's Glasnost!!!" prompts Maggie, "Openess, a chat!"
"Oh! Glasnost? Like friendship? Cat, I Dulac Dat!
I'm not just hopin' - it's my biggest dream
That the famous Moss Cow'll share a bucket of cream!"
Giant white pelicans with radar direction
Lift Dulac Cat and the kitty collection.
Eight graceful wings stretch and swoon and swoop
And away they all soar with The Whirl Class troop!
Over the snow covered steppes they fly
Like four downy cat-a-ma-rans skimming the sky.
"It's all in a name! I am Piccalilli Pel I Can!
I can fly you there and I can fly you back again!"
The cats sink their claws into the flitty, fluffy down
And Wink nervously wrinkles her whiskers to a frown.
"My wings are strong. I'm the sky's Peter Pan!
You needn't worry, Wink," sooths Piccalilli Pel I Can.
"Are we there yet?" begs Chu-Chut as she looks for shore.
"Land-a-Goshen! What a notion! Hear my feathers roar!
Calm your pretty noggins, settle back and rest;
Ax Professor P.H.Dee to quote poetry and jest!"

Smoothing his jacket, Rhatt turns up his meow,
"Doctor, doctor, doctor, tell us all about this cow!
Does her milk turn to cheese?
Can she jump through a hoop?"
"Yeah!" Dulac Cat chimes. "Give us da scoop!
Does she wear moss on her head or moss on her tail?
Does she pull moss past her eyes or out of a pail?
Will Moss Cow like us? Will she invite us in?
If we dribble milk, will she wipe our chin?"
Tugging at his britches, pulling them up for size,
And clearing his throat, the good doctor replies:
"I'm not the kind of cat who'd kill curiosity!
Curiosity is our legacy, you see!!
Mossy may surpass your wildest anticipation,
But the greatest celebration is your own imagination!"
The poet's words are spoken and the cats begin to purr;
Shivering, Dulac sputters, "I'm glad we're wearing fur!"
Wink and Peaches play pat-a-cake and singsong to Dulac Cat,
"Answer if you will and end our little spat!
Does Mossy sit on a tuffet? Does she eat curds and whey?
Does she sit on a mossy pillow? Snooze away the day?"

"Girls!!   You ax too many questions!!"
Snorts flustered Big Mamou!
"So what, if her star eyes twinkle a Jello-yellow hue?
Differences can be delightful! Don't be a loup-ga-rou!"*
The cats sail on, the sun sinks low;
Whispy ducks and dragons wave a soft hello.
Strong wings lurch cat-er-corner, Lilli circles wide;
Tightening their seat belts, the cats crouch side by side.
"An ounce of doubt and you're already out!
Put a smile on your face - this is no time to pout!"

loup-ga-rou   *werewolf*

Lilli descends through the clouds, the cats take a peek;
A feast for tired eyes, enough to make the cats weak!
"Well, twitter my whiskers!" Rhatt says with a shout;
"Talk about magnificent! Moss Cow can dish it out!"
The earth below lay close and big and cold and shimmering;
Palaces and castles rose gossamer, gold and glimmering!
The moon dangled above like a queen's crystal ladle;
The hills swaddled the town like black Russian sable.

"Now I'm Dulac, dat Cajun Cat,
Dat Cajun Cat from down Dulac!
Da garlic in da basket above Mamou's kitchen zink*
Are big as Newton figs and onions plump and pink!
But jumpin' jilly whiskers, just get a load of dat!
Golden onions on da rooftops and garlic twice as fat!"
"Dulac!" prompts Magnolia. "Watch the words you choose!
With the Magnificent Moss Cow, use your T's and Q's!
Say This and That and These and Those!
NOT Dis and Dat and Deez and Dose!!"
"G-a-a-w! Dey do t'ings grand!" Dulac wipes her brow;
"Wit' garlic big as d-dis, whatcha t'ink about da cow?
Sha! Nicholas tossed his cookies when da scarlet flag unfurled!
Creamland is not jus' a country, I t'ink it is a whirl!"

zink   *sink*

Auntie Litter holds each kitty
As Dulac sings a ditty:
"T-this is not a rehearsal nor a silly soap commercial!
It's as gutsy-look-'em-in-the-eye real as can be!
From t-the moment we set foot and point our little snoot
Toward the palace to see what we can see. . ."
Interrupting, Auntie Litter adds her pitter:
"We'll be challenging our courage,
So I brought along some porridge
To give us strength and shore up our dignity!"

At dusk the giant pelicans gently all touch down;
A feather light landing in Moss Cow's hometown.
"T-t-this is the moment," smiles Dulac,
"We've been waiting for!
Who wants to be t-the first to knock upon da door?"
Tux taps up the steps, dashing ahead of the pack
And grabs the brass knocker and gives it a WHACK!
He twirls his umbrella and tips his jazz hat,
Then kicks up his heels boppin' Da-Dulac-Dat!

The cats hear a snicker - they turn with a whiff;
A husky little dog muffles his cheer with a sniff.
"Who dat say dey gonna top Tux Cat
Dancin' Da-Dulac-Dat on t-the big red mat?"
Dulac eyes the little dog, but her words are for the pack.
Out of Piccalilli's pouch, T-Bone pulls a burlap sack.
"Come on," pleads T-Bone, "Let's don't be a boo-ga-loo!*
Let's toss butinsky here a hush puppy or two."
T-Bone flexes his muscles and stammers a minute,
"Take this *peace* of bread with a *peace* of boudin* in it!"
"Khah-rah-sho sahs-sees-kee! Spahs-see-bah!"*
Doggie smacks his lips!
"He likes it! He likes it! Hot dog!" T-Bone quips.
"And I brought an extra *peace* for our magnificent host;
Moss Cow, come out and serve us a *peace* of milk toast!"
There's a clicking of the lock in the big red door;
A bright sliver of light shoots across the porch floor!
"Meow in there! Or should we say moo?"
Dulac Cat sings, "Can you give us a clue?"
With a wooden spoon Dulac stirs a low commotion;
Then on her glad left paw she tests the magic lotion.
"Here's a *peace* of catnip mixed wit' Miss'ippi mud
To sparkle up your milk and sweeten your cud -
A *peace* of which rubbed on the nose of a cow
Turns you into a cat and your moo to a meow!"
The little dog laughed to hear such a tune,
Wondering what kind of dish was stirred with the spoon!
All the world is silent, the cats' noses all twitch;
The excitement sharpens their purring a pitch.
"Will the Moss Cow meow or will she moo?"
"And if she meows, will she meow like we do?"

boo-ga-loo   *booger*
boudin   *sausage*
Khah-rah-sho sahs-sees-kee! Spahs-see bah!
Good sausage!   Thank You!

"Does she use mousse or did she turn a moose loose?"
"You ask too much!" sighs Maggie. "Don't be silly-willy!"
She flits up the steps as the wind whips wild and chilly.
"YOO-HOO!!
Here's a *peace* of yarn with a sweater stuck to it.
For warmth every winter, this sweater will do it!"
"Why doesn't Mossy come out to play - right now?"
Chu-Chut wonders out loud,
Then sings a magnificent meow for the magnificent cow!
Then dawdling and dragging her brown paper sack,
And nibbling a sugar beignet* for a snack,
Chu-Chut lifts her paw. "Here's a *peace* of praline.*
Trade ya' for a saucer of sweet Moss Cow cream?"
Now up the steps Le☆n shakes with a bound,
Humming a glad tune about a sad hound.
Ne☆n Le☆n glows far brighter than ever!
Then he brightens some more as he thinks of a clever
Gift he can give to the cow that will never
Get lost or tarnish with the passage of time!
The stars on his whiskers ring out like a chime!
On a musical 'paws,' with his rock 'n roll claws
He lifts one star - the brightest by far!!
"I'll give you a lucky star if you'll just show your face!
You can spill all your milk without leaving a trace!"
On the latch, Le☆n hangs the glowing rock star,
Which glows bright as his smile,
Then glows brighter by far!!

beignet   doughnut
praline   pecan candy

"What a prize," Wink sighs, blinking her eyes.
"I brought a *peace* of ribbon from my spring bonnet -
Take the ribbon and the bonnet and the japonica on it!"
Auntie Litter yells, "Mossy!
I don't mean to sound bossy,
But put this peach pie on the highest shelf
So you can eat it all by yourself!!"
Big Mamou's eyes are glowing - her confidence growing!
"While I had my apron on with planty t'ings to bake,
I stirred up a surprise, how you call a *peace* of cake!
And I brought along some peppers, some sweet, some hot,
To sizzle up the gumbo in this old iron pot!"
The little dog is smiling and his nose begins to wiggle;
Then he grins and he grins again, till out pops a giggle!
"This doggie," purrs Maggie, "really thinks he's tough!"
"He is!!" Snips Dulac! "He's really hot stuff!!"
The cats stand up on tippy-toes
As the door swings open wide!
Hot Stuff snuggles close to Dulac -
There's no place else to hide!
WHAM BAM! KUDZU KAZAM! PLINK-A-DINK! WHADU WHATAM??
The door swings open wider, the cats all shout, "SHAZAM!!"
There's yakking and clacking and stomping and cracking,
And jawing and gnawing and romping and smacking!!

"Golly-jolly snollygoster!* What you make of dat?"
Words stick in Dulac's throat. "It's a shorely not a cat!
Dat noise would startle a wizard and swizzle your gizzard!
Pump up da balloon on t-the throat of a lizard!!"
Dulac inches closer and then she forks her brow,
"S-h-h-h-h! I don't hear a moo and I don't see a cow!"

snollygoster   *goblin*

Hoisting his trousers, P.H.Dee come out smokin'!
"Here's a *peace* of my mind, and I'm not just a-jokin'!
A sip of milk will quench this highfalutin foofaraw*
And we will leave in peace,
Quick as this cat can lick his paw!!''

foofaraw   *fuss*

"Pooyie! Sha!*
What magnificent t'ing can I do
To make da Moss Cow moo?"
Dulac pulls out her fiddle, the circle is complete.
The cats all gather round her and begin to tap their feet.
    "Now I'm Dulac, dat Cajun Cat,
    Dat Cajun Cat from down Dulac!
    A *peace* of Fly High music,
    Straight from t-this left paw cat,
    Moss Cow, come out an' join us!
    Sing and dance Da-Dulac-Dat!"
Over the diddle-diddle fiddle, she pulls the red-hot bow,
The cats swing foot loose, now giddy-up, cats, go!
  "Come out and celebrate with The Whirl Class Cats!
  We're struttin' our stuffin' and tossed in our hats!
  Come on! Roll out the mat! You can Dulac Dat!
  And we will pat your back and dance Da-Dulac-Dat!"
Mossy peeps through the door at the cats' Golden Horde,*
Listening as Dulac plays the last Whirl Class chord.
Then she shoves a big bucket of milk with her hoof;
At the sight of the milk the cats howl through the roof!
Spilling over doggie's ears is a ten inch grin;
Then Hot Stuff pops a grin that bobbles over his chin.
The cats are bowing, lips smacking the thick golden cream,
"Is this real?" Auntie beams, "or only a dream?"
"Oh! The milk's really real! And so is the cow!!
She likes us!! She likes us!!
T-the milk proves it right now!"
Hot Stuff scrooches close, within the cat pack,
And wagging his tail, gives the bucket a WHACK!

Pooyie! Sha!   *Phooey! Cats!*
Horde   *throng*

The gang sings out a chorus of jubilant praise,
Though they don't see the cow, their voices they raise:
   "Thank you, your Royal Highness!
   Can you hear us in there?
   Your milk is a *masterpeace*
   Beyond all compare!!
   Hail!   Hail the milk!   Hail!
   Bubbling up from the big brass pail!
   Hail!   Hail the milk!   Hail!
   Sparkling fresh from the big glas grail!"

The cats are now shouting, "It's time to depart!
The last gift we're giving is a PEACE OF OUR HEART!"
Piccalilli's feathers quiver white as baby fleece.
"Speak now," Rhatt growls frankly,
"OR FOREVER HOLD YOUR PEACE!!"
The cats jump aboard Pel I Can, ready to fly;
All comfy, all cozy, not a tear in their eye.
Chasing feathers and fur across the airport,
The little dog laughed to see such a sport!
Trotting as fast as he can, to his paws gives a boost,
And lands smack in Mamou's fat lap for a roost!
They circle Moss City, buzzing cathedrals of gold,
Looking down on the courtyard, when lo and behold!
The square is a-dazzle like a Mardi Gras torch!!
The Magnificent Cow has strolled out on the porch!!
From the catbird seat, Dulac warms up her fiddle,
As Moss Cow explores the cats' Whirl Class riddle!
Mossy chomps on the bread and stomps the purr-tater;
She chews the praline and samples the 'gator!
She pulls on the hat, sticks her head through the cake;
Hooks the yarn on her horn and gives it a shake!
She steppes in the pie and tests the mud potion;
Then brushes it on with a magnificent motion!
She twirls the umbrella and pins on the star;
The most magnificent star, the cow thinks, by far!!

Moss Cow sips the hot gumbo and makes happy faces;
Then lets out a moo and kicks over her traces!!
The moon hovers above her like a big silver scoop;
She belts out a yodel and jumps right through the loop!
Moss Cow lands on all fours! PURR KLUNK in a cloud!
Without batting an eyelash! For cryin' out loud!
A quick swish of her tail flips the Big Dipper,
Splashing milk on the moon and sloshing her slipper!
She jumps over Venus, then she jumps over Mars,
Plays bounce with the sun and juggles the stars!!
On the rim of tomorrow, Moss Cow greets a new day,
Dancin' Da-Dulac-Dat along the Great Milky Way!!!
The whirligig cats gaze out through the blue;
Goose bumpy, nose tingly, hearing the cow's jazzy moo!
Now feathers and ruffles and banners are flyin';
Balloons bobbin', heads noddin', cats' paws hi-fivin'!
Dulac gives each cat a big pat-on-the-back,
"Moss Cow's singin' an' dancin'! I Dulac Dat!!"
Eyes twinkling with wonder, the little dog yapped.
Curled deep in the down, the kitties all napped.
The cow disappears through the light of the moon;
And the cats all sail home to the tune of a loon.
Dawn sets out a breakfast of peaches and cream,
A sweet celebration of a magnificent dream!

International Standard Book Number   0-944512-01-1
Library of Congress Catalog Card Number   89-063795